Skimper-Scamper

Skimper-Scamper

Jeff Newell

Illustrated by Barbara Hranilovich

Green Light Readers
Harcourt, Inc.

Orlando Austin New York San Diego Toronto London

"Let's play outside later,"
said Lisa's mom.

"Okay," said Lisa.
Lisa got her crayons and made a small blue mouse.

Then—**skimper-scamper**—
the mouse ran off the paper!

The mouse grabbed Lisa's jump rope.
"Stop!" said Lisa. "You're making a mess."

"No way," said the mouse.
Lisa got her crayons and made a medium yellow cat.

Then—**skimper scamper**—
the cat ran off the paper!

The cat and mouse had fun with Lisa's paints.

"Stop!" said Lisa. "You're making a mess."

"No way," said the cat.
Lisa got her crayons and made a large black dog.

Then—**skimper scamper**—
the dog ran off the paper!

The dog, the cat, and the mouse had fun playing ball.

"Stop!" said Lisa. "You're making a mess."

"No way," said the dog.
"If you all clean up, I'll make you a surprise,"
said Lisa.

"Okay," said the dog, the cat,
and the mouse.

Lisa's mom knocked on the door.
"Are you ready to go outside?" she asked.
"Just a minute," said Lisa.

Lisa gave the dog, the cat, and
the mouse their surprise.

"Now, let's play!"

Collage Animals

You can make your own animals—
just like Lisa!

WHAT YOU'LL NEED

ribbons

scissors

cloth scraps

construction paper

feathers

buttons

glitter

markers

crayons

glue

1. Choose an animal that you like.

2. Use all sorts of different craft supplies to make your animal. Then glue everything together.

3. After you finish your animal collage, write a story about your animal.

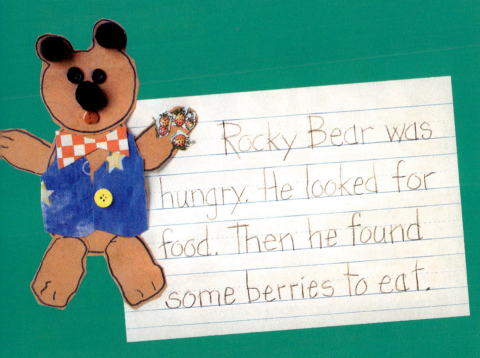

Rocky Bear was hungry. He looked for food. Then he found some berries to eat.

Share your animal and your story with a friend!

Meet the Illustrator

Barbara Hranilovich based the dog, the cat, and the mouse in *Skimper-Scamper* on animals her son drew. She hopes that your drawings will give you lots of ideas for your own stories!

Barbara Hranilovich

www.HarcourtBooks.com

First Green Light Readers edition 2005
Green Light Readers is a trademark of Harcourt, Inc., registered in
the United States of America and/or other jurisdictions.

Library of Congress Cataloging-in-Publication Data
Newell, Jeff (Jeff A.)
Skimper-scamper/Jeff Newell; illustrated by Barbara Hranilovich.
p. cm.
"Green Light Readers."
Summary: When the mouse, cat, and dog that she has drawn run off the paper
and make a mess of her room, Lisa must find a way to stop them.
[1. Drawing—Fiction. 2. Mice—Fiction. 3. Cats—Fiction. 4. Dogs—Fiction.
5. Orderliness—Fiction.] I. Hranilovich, Barbara J., ill. II. Title. III. Series:
Green Light reader.
PZ7.N47915Ski 2005
[E]—dc22   2003026931
ISBN 0-15-205166-X
ISBN 0-15-205165-1 pb

A C E G H F D B
A C E G H F D B (pb)

Ages 5–7
Grades: 1–2
Guided Reading Level: G–I
Reading Recovery Level: 15–16

Green Light Readers
For the reader who's ready to GO!

Five Tips to Help Your Child Become a Great Reader

1. Get involved. Reading aloud to and with your child is just as important as encouraging your child to read independently.

2. Be curious. Ask questions about what your child is reading.

3. Make reading fun. Allow your child to pick books on subjects that interest her or him.

4. Words are everywhere—not just in books. Practice reading signs, packages, and cereal boxes with your child.

5. Set a good example. Make sure your child sees YOU reading.

Why Green Light Readers Is the Best Series for Your New Reader

• Created exclusively for beginning readers by some of the biggest and brightest names in children's books

• Reinforces the reading skills your child is learning in school

• Encourages children to read—and finish—books by themselves

• Offers extra enrichment through fun, age-appropriate activities unique to each story

• Incorporates characteristics of the Reading Recovery program used by educators

• Developed with Harcourt School Publishers and credentialed educational consultants

Daniel's Mystery Egg
Alma Flor Ada/G. Brian Karas

Animals on the Go
Jessica Brett/Richard Cowdrey

Marco's Run
Wesley Cartier/Reynold Ruffins

Digger Pig and the Turnip
Caron Lee Cohen/Christopher Denise

Tumbleweed Stew
Susan Stevens Crummel/Janet Stevens

The Chick That Wouldn't Hatch
Claire Daniel/Lisa Campbell Ernst

Splash!
Ariane Dewey/Jose Aruego

Get That Pest!
Erin Douglas/Wong Herbert Yee

A Place for Nicholas
Lucy Floyd/David McPhail

Why the Frog Has Big Eyes
Betsy Franco/Joung Un Kim

I Wonder
Tana Hoban

A Bed Full of Cats
Holly Keller

The Fox and the Stork
Gerald McDermott

Try Your Best
Robert McKissack/Joe Cepeda

Lucy's Quiet Book
Angela Shelf Medearis/Lisa Campbell Ernst

Tomás Rivera
Jane Medina/Edward Martinez

Boots for Beth
Alex Moran/Lisa Campbell Ernst

Catch Me If You Can!
Bernard Most

The Very Boastful Kangaroo
Bernard Most

Skimper-Scamper
Jeff Newell/Barbara Hranilovich

Farmers Market
Carmen Parks/Edward Martinez

Shoe Town
Janet Stevens/Susan Stevens Crummel

The Enormous Turnip
Alexei Tolstoy/Scott Goto

Where Do Frogs Come From?
Alex Vern

The Purple Snerd
Rozanne Lanczak Williams/Mary GrandPré

Did You See Chip?
Wong Herbert Yee/Laura Ovresat

Look for more Green Light Readers wherever books are sold!